Crocodile Listens

BY
APRIL PULLEY SAYRE

PICTURES BY
JoELLEN McALLISTER STAMMEN

GREENWILLOW BOOKS • *An Imprint of HarperCollinsPublishers*

*Special thanks to Dr. Christopher J. Raxworthy
of the American Museum of Natural History and
to Dr. James Perran Ross of the IUCN Crocodile
Specialist Group and the Florida Museum of
Natural History for their scientific guidance.*

Library of Congress Cataloging-in-Publication Data

Sayre, April Pulley.
Crocodile Listens / by April Pulley Sayre ; pictures by JoEllen McAllister Stammen.
    p.   cm.
"Greenwillow Books."
Summary: As other animals walk, gallop or trot by, a hungry crocodile
lies quietly in the sand, listening for a very special sound from her
nesting place. Includes factual information about Nile crocodiles.
ISBN 0-688-16504-4 (trade). ISBN 0-688-16505-2 (lib. bdg.)
1. Nile crocodile—Juvenile fiction. [1. Nile crocodile—Fiction. 2. Crocodiles—Fiction.
3. Animals—Fiction. 4. Africa—Fiction.] I. McAllister Stammen, Jo Ellen, ill. II. Title.
PZ10.3.S2777 Cr 2001   [E]—dc21   00-050335

For my sister Lydia —A. P. S.

To the Hearer of my heart —J.M.S.

Like an ancient dinosaur
with scraggly teeth,
Crocodile lies in the sand.
Birds call. Rivers run.
Baboons file past.
And all the while, Crocodile listens.

Thump, thump, thump . . .

A thunder of thumps pounds the grassy ground.

A herd of giraffes gallops past.

But Crocodile just looks and listens.

Tromp, tromp, tromp.

Warthog toes trot. Warthogs are delicious
for dinner. Yet all the while, sun-warmed
Crocodile simply lies and listens.

Croak, croak, croak!
comes a small frog's call.
A frog would make
a very good snack.
Crocodile's mouth is open.
She has not eaten for weeks. . . .

Yet for some reason,
she only listens.

Scratch, scratch, scratch.
Monitor lizard makes his move.
He starts to dig in the sand.
Snap! go Crocodile's jaws.
Her tail lashes. Something
secret is hidden below.

Chi! Chi! Chi!

cries Thick-knee, the bird.

She runs as Crocodile starts to pace.

Crocodile isn't a friendly neighbor.

But she is helpful.

She keeps egg-eating lizards away.

Whump, whump, whump!
Crocodile's walking feet thump.
In the sand, tiny ears hear her steps.
Whump, WHUMP!

Underground, baby crocodiles call.

They are hatching.

And they need their mama's help!

Beeeeyo, beeeeyo, beeeeyo!

cry the babies.

Will their mother hear them?

Whump, WHUMP!

Crocodile's feet are loud.

Weaverbirds chatter.

Harroooo! the elephants trumpet.

Crocodile stops.

She turns toward the mound.

Beeeeyo, beeeeyo, beeeeyo!
cry the babies.
The sand seems to sing
with their calls.
Now, at last, Crocodile
hears them.

Beeeeyo, beeeeyo,
the babies croon. Their mother digs.
Scoop. Push. Scrape.
Scoop. Push. Scrape.
By morning, the babies are free!

But wait . . .

Eeeeep . . . eeeeep . . . eeeeep,

cries one tiny baby.

It's trapped inside its shell!

Crocodile grasps the egg

in her powerful jaws . . .

and gently closes down.

Kaak . . . kaak . . . kaak . . .

The shell slowly cracks.

Is it crushed?

No! A baby's snout appears.

Beeyo. Urp! **Beeyo.** Urp!

the baby calls,

breaking free from its shell.

Beeyo! Urp! **Beeyo!** Urp!
the babies call.
They squirm and squeak in the sand.
But meanwhile a mongoose
is slipping through the shadows. . . .
Danger is at hand.

Yip! **Urp!** Yip!
the babies squeal.
To a mongoose, they are morsels of meat.
Good thing Crocodile is watching closely.
She scoops them up among her teeth.

Safe in her mouth, the babies ride to the Nile River. They start to feed. Crocodile snaps up fish, a long-awaited feast.

Croak, croak, croak!
comes a small frog's call.
There's room for one bite more.
But not now.

Crocodile has
babies to tend,
and they have
the whole Nile to explore. . . .

MORE ABOUT THE NILE CROCODILE

Nile crocodiles *(Crocodylus niloticus)* live in and along lakes, rivers, and swamps in Africa and on the island of Madagascar. They are big animals, averaging about sixteen feet or more in length. Usually they are big eaters, too. They hunt and eat antelope, buffalo, young hippos, fish, and frogs.

The female crocodile lays anywhere from forty to sixty eggs in a hole about one and a half feet deep that she has dug in the sandy shore of a river or lake. There she stands guard, not even allowing herself to hunt, until after the babies hatch three months later. The male crocodile is generally not involved in protecting the eggs or raising the young. During the mother crocodile's long wait, she tries to keep egg-eating predators such as hyenas, monitor lizards, and mongooses away from her nesting area. Other egg-laying animals such as turtles and waterbirds take advantage of this and frequently will make their own nests nearby.

When the baby crocodiles start to hatch, they begin calling. Some scientists believe the young crocodiles feel the vibrations from their mother's footsteps and call to respond. Either way, when the mother hears the babies' high-pitched chirps, she digs down into the sand to reach them. Usually the eggs hatch without problems. But sometimes the mother gently cracks an eggshell with her teeth to help a baby get out.

When all the eggs have hatched, the mother crocodile carries her young to the water, where they swim together. The mother crocodile breaks her three-month fast by eating fish or other large prey. The hatchlings catch and eat insects, spiders, and small frogs. For their first few weeks, the babies will remain close to their mother, often resting on her back.